A LITTLE SPOT OF SADNESS

Written & Illustrated by Diane Alber

To my children, Ryan and Anna,

Always remember you have the power
to CALM a SADNESS SPOT!

This book belongs to:

_____

_____

_____

Hi! I'm a PEACEFUL SPOT!

And this BLUE SPOT is a SADNESS SPOT.

A **SADNESS SPOT** can show up when someone is feeling upset, disappointed, or if they experience loss.

SADNESS is one of the many emotions we can
experience every day. Other emotions are
ANXIETY and ANGER, too!
We all have these emotions inside of us.
But we feel the best when we are able to CALM them down
into a PEACEFUL SPOT.

Sadness   Anger   Anxiety

You will see both SMALL and LARGE SPOTS of
SADNESS. Having your SADNESS SPOT around is okay,
but when it stays TOO LONG or becomes TOO BIG,
it doesn't make you feel very good.

That's why I'm here to show you how to recognize when someone's SADNESS SPOT shows up and how to help them find a PEACEFUL SPOT!

I'll also show you how to manage your own SADNESS SPOT, too!

A SADNESS SPOT is unique because it is one of the few emotions that other people can help you with. That's why I want to show you how to SPOT it!

CRYING is one of the ways a SADNESS SPOT releases energy, which can help you feel better. It can also show you when a person is feeling down, so you can go and help them find their PEACEFUL SPOT.

It's also important to know that a SADNESS SPOT
may be there even if someone is not CRYING.
You can look at their body language, too.

If you see someone FROWNING or MOPING,
their SADNESS SPOT is definitely nearby.

This person could use a friend.

LONELINESS can cause your SADNESS SPOT
to get bigger, too.

If you see someone who could use a friend, ask them if
they are okay and be there to listen.
If you have experienced what they are going
through, let them know they are not alone
and you are there for them.

You are CALMING their SADNESS SPOT
with EMPATHY.

It can be common to see an ANXIETY SPOT with a SADNESS SPOT. When a new kid arrives to class, they may be worried and sad at the same time. You can help them feel more welcome by saying hello and introducing them to your friends.

You are CALMING their SADNESS SPOT with COMPASSION.

A SADNESS SPOT can be a little sneaky!
Like when it shows up before you decide how to react
to the problem.

Sometimes it takes the help of others to see it's only a tiny
problem that can easily be fixed.

You are CALMING their SADNESS SPOT
with TEAMWORK.

You might also see a SADNESS SPOT appear when someone has lost a pet, friend, or family member.

Being there to give them a hug and talk about the happy times they shared with that person or pet, can help them feel the LOVE that will always be in their heart.

You are CALMING their SADNESS SPOT with LOVE.

Sometimes you might see a SADNESS SPOT show up when someone misses a loved one who is far away.

Having a friend to have fun with can really help!

You are CALMING their SADNESS SPOT with FRIENDSHIP.

There are ways to CALM your own SADNESS SPOT, too.
Some days you just feel SAD, and you aren't really sure why.
When you feel like being alone or no one is there to
comfort you, music, drawing, and writing can help
relax your mind!

You are CALMING YOUR SADNESS SPOT with CREATIVITY.

If your SADNESS SPOT won't go away,
I have a trick you can try!

Look at your hand... Now imagine one
BLUE SPOT and one GREEN SPOT on your palm.

Just like this!

Repeat after me:

Circle the SPOTS in the middle of your palm,
count the swirls down to CALM.
Around and around, and around twice more.
One, then two, then three, then four.
Each time you trace around the SPOTS,
take a deep breath to CALM your thoughts.

I'm so glad to see that you have learned how to CALM down SADNESS SPOTS!

Always remember our little trick!

Circle the SPOTS in the middle of your palm,
count the swirls down to CALM.
Around and around, and around twice more.
One, then two, then three, then four.
Each time you trace around the SPOTS,
take a deep breath to CALM your thoughts.

You can imagine your own spots or cut them out of construction paper and place them on your palm. You can also get real SPOT stickers in bulk on my website: www.dianealber.com